HOW SPIDER SAVED HALLOWEEN

BY ROBERT KRAUS

SCHOLASTIC BOOK SERVICES

NEW YORK • TORONTO • LONDON • AUCKLAND • SYDNEY • TOKYO

For Pamela, Billy, and Bruce

Copyright © 1973 by Robert Kraus. This edition is published by Scholastic Book Services, a division of Scholastic Magazines, Inc., by arrangement with Parents' Magazine Press.

1st printing .... September 1974

Printed in the U.S.A.

It was Halloween eve and, try as I might,
I couldn't think of a good disguise.

No matter what costume I tried on,
I still looked like me.

I went to see my good friend Ladybug, hoping she might help.
She was on the porch, carving a jack-o'-lantern with Fly.

"I hope I'm not intruding," I said.

"You're always intruding," said Fly.

"Hush, Fly," said Ladybug. "Come in, Spider. You're always welcome."

"Thank you," I replied.
I never felt that Fly liked me. But Ladybug liked me enough for two!

"Why aren't you wearing your costume?"
asked Ladybug.

"Because my problem is that no matter what
I put on I still look like me."

"That is a problem," said Fly.

"We'll solve it," said Ladybug. "Let's go inside,
and Fly and I will get into our costumes.
It will help us get ideas."

"Good," I said.

Fly went into the bathroom.
Minutes later he came out in a beard and cap.

"Who am I?" asked Fly.

"Santa Claus," I replied.

"Wrong," said Fly. "I'm one of the seven dwarfs."

Then Ladybug excused herself and went into
the bathroom to change into her costume.
Minutes later she emerged.

"What am I?" asked Ladybug.

"A witch," I said.

"Correct," said Ladybug.

"Now for you," said Ladybug.
She dressed me up in ladies' clothes.

"You still look like you," said Fly.

"Still looks like himself," said Ladybug.

"Looks even more like himself," said Fly.

A cowboy suit wasn't much better.

We all put our heads together to think of a
costume that would *really* disguise me. Suddenly
there was a sickening *SQUASH* from the porch.

We all ran outside to see what it was.
Ladybug's jack-o'-lantern was wrecked!
Two bullies with baseball bats were hooting
and running away.

Ladybug burst into tears. "Our beautiful pumpkin!" she cried.

"And it's too late to get another," moaned Fly. "Halloween is ruined!"

"It's true," I said. "Halloween without a pumpkin just isn't Halloween."
I stopped feeling sorry for myself and started feeling sorry for my friends.

Then I got an idea.
"Color me orange!" I said.
They colored me orange.

While they were coloring me orange,
I cut up a piece of green construction paper.

"Paste this on my head," I said.

Fly got the paste jar.
Ladybug did the pasting.

Then I took a black marker and drew lines on
myself and blacked out my front teeth.

"You're a pumpkin!" they both exclaimed.
"Halloween isn't spoiled after all!"

"You're darn tootin' " I said. "On to trick or treat!"

We tricked-or-treated all over the neighborhood, and everyone gave us lots of treats and admired our costumes. Especially the walking, talking pumpkin.

At last our bags were full
and we headed home—
when who should we see coming
down the street but the two bullies
who had smashed the jack-o'-lantern. They were heading
our way with cans of shaving cream.

"They'll spray us with shaving cream!" cried Ladybug.

"They'll steal our trick or treats," moaned Fly.

"No they won't," I said. "They're bullies, and bullies are cowards. Quick. Hide behind this bush."

Just as the bullies passed by,
I jumped out
and screamed, "Boo!"

The bullies dropped their shaving cream
and ran away screaming, "A pumpkin ghost!
A pumpkin ghost! Save us! Save us!"

We went back to Ladybug's house and counted our loot. Ladybug planted a kiss on my cheek and Fly shook my hand.

"Because you saved Halloween," said Ladybug.

"I must admit you did it," said Fly. "You saved Halloween."

I guess I had. And I was very happy to have saved Halloween for my two dear friends, Fly and Ladybug.

The End